This verse version of
Jack and the Beanstalk
is adapted from the one titled
*The History of Mother Twaddle and the
Marvelous Achievements of her Son Jack,*
written by B.A.T.
that appeared in London in 1807,
published by J. Harris,
corner of St. Paul's Churchyard.

*The assistance of the
Osborne Collection of the Toronto Public Library
is gratefully acknowledged.*

JACK
and the
BEANSTALK

For another Jack

Copyright © 1974 by Paul Galdone

All rights reserved. Published in the United States by HMH Books, an imprint of Houghton Mifflin Harcourt Publishing Company. Originally published in hardcover in the United States by Clarion Books, an imprint of Houghton Mifflin Harcourt Publishing Company, 1974.

For information about permission to reproduce selections from this book, write to Permissions, Houghton Mifflin Harcourt Publishing Company, 215 Park Avenue South, New York, New York 10003.

www.hmhbooks.com

The Library of Congress Cataloging-in-Publication data is on file.

ISBN: 978-0-544-06665-6 paper over board
ISBN: 978-0-89919-085-3 paperback

Manufactured in Mexico
RDT 10 9 8 7 6 5 4 3 2

4500451639

JACK
and the
BEANSTALK

A FOLK TALE CLASSIC

Paul Galdone

Houghton Mifflin Harcourt
Boston   New York

As Old Mother Twaddle
Was sweeping her floor,
She found a new sixpence
Under the door.
And as she surveyed it
With exquisite pleasure,
She called her son Jack
To look at her treasure.

 will comb thee, and wash thee,

    And make thee quite spruce.

Thou shalt go to the fair

    And buy us a goose.

For of all the good things,

    I vow and protest,

A fat, tasty goose

    Is the thing I love best.''

When Old Mother Twaddle
Had sent Jack to the fair,
She hastened with onions
And sage to prepare
A savory stuffing
For the delicate treat,
And thought with what glee
Of the tidbits she'd eat.

When Jack reached the fair
  And round him was staring
A peddler cried out,
  "Buy this bean for a farthing.
It possesses such virtues
  That sure as a gun,
Tomorrow it will grow
  Near as high as the sun!"

Jack bought it for sixpence
   Then went to his Mother,
Who at sight of the bean
   Made a terrible pother.
She gave him a scolding
   And slapped both his hands,
For having presumed
   Not to mind her commands.

Jack went to the garden
    And took up his spade,
Then put the rare bean
    In the hole he had made,
Expecting to find
    This great wonder of wonders
As tall as a tree
    To make up for his blunders.

Next morning Jack rose
    To view the large bean,
When to his surprise,
    E'en the top was not seen!
It made a long ladder
    As strong as a rope,
And Jack soon climbed on high
    Full of joy and of hope.

He knocked at the door
Of a very grand place;
A damsel came to it
With a cap all of lace.
"Oh! Pray go from hence!"
Cried this maid in a fright,
"For a giant lives here,
And he'll eat you this night!"

Jack begged to come in
      With so winning an air
That she promised to hide him
      And pointed out where.
He no sooner had hidden
      Than the door opened wide,
And in stalked the Giant
      With a very long stride.

Then the Monster roared out,
   "Fe, fi, fo, fan!
I smell the breath
   Of an Englishman!
If he be alive,
   Or if he be dead,
I'll grind his bones
   To make my bread!"

"Oh wait, my dear Giant,
    First drink some strong wine,
Then on that dainty
    You may afterwards dine."
He seized a large cup
    And tippled so deep,
Then he tumbled down flat
    And fell fast asleep.

Soon as Jack saw him fall,
He crept from the bed,
Then snatched a large knife
And chopped off his head.
Thus he killed this great man,
As he loudly did snore,
And never again
Was a Giant seen more.

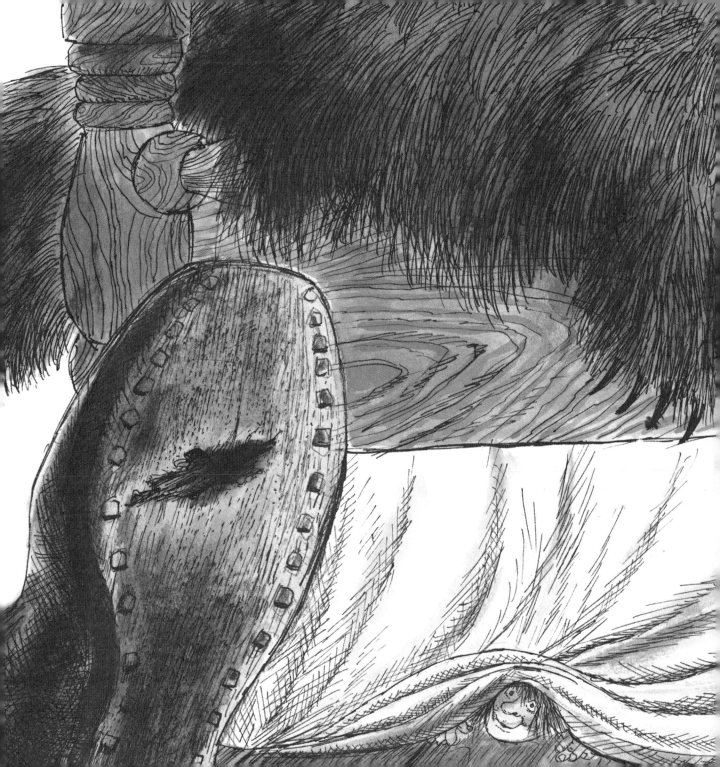

Jack sent for his Mother
    To come up and dine,
With a promise of goose
    And a bottle of wine.
And as she did eat it
    With excessive delight,
She approved of his bargain
    And said he'd done right.

Jack sent for a parson,
   As he had a great mind
To marry the damsel,
   Who was willing and kind.
The Parson came soon
   And made her Jack's Wife,
And they lived very happy
   To the end of their life.

Here Jack, and his Wife,
　　And his Mother are seen
All dancing a jig
　　Round the wonderful bean.